D1335392

Greetings, People of Earth:

It's me, Carly! And this is the second installment in the iHistory of iCarly. By now you know that iCarly is a total Web phenomenon . . . Wow! Phenomenon . . . My vocabulary has really improved since I started doing a weekly show!

In spite of that, I have to remind myself that anything could happen. I mean, iCarly started by accident, and it could end the same way. The studio could suddenly go dark . . . Of course, that would probably mean my brother Spencer had overloaded the electrical circuits with one of his art projects and blown out the fuses! Still, I like to think that whatever happens, this book filled with really great photos will keep you in the loop of all the iCarly madness! So grab a smoothie (may I recommend the Blueberry Banana Blitz?) and prepare to laugh—just try not to have a mouthful of smoothie when you do, because if it comes out your nose, it's going to hurt . . . trust me on this one.

And don't forget: Keep watching iCarly—bye for now!

iWanna Stay

iWanna Stay

Adapted by Laurie McElroy

Part 1: Based on the episode "iSpy a Mean Teacher"
Written By Steven Molaro

Part 2: Based on the episode "iWanna Stay with Spencer"
Written By Arthur Gradstein

Based on the TV Series "iCarly" Created By
Dan Schneider

SIMON AND SCHUSTER

SIMON AND SCHUSTER

First published in Great Britain in 2009 by Simon & Schuster UK Ltd,
1st Floor, 222 Gray's Inn Road, London WC1X 8HB
A CBS COMPANY

Originally published in the USA by Scholastic, 2009

© 2009 Viacom International Inc. All Rights Reserved.
Nickelodeon, Nickelodeon iCarly, and all related titles,
logos and characters are trademarks of Viacom International Inc.
All rights reserved, including the right to reproduce this book
or portions thereof in any form whatsoever

A CIP catalogue record for this book is available from the British Library

ISBN 978-1-84738-626-7

10 9 8 7 6 5 4 3 2 1

Printed by CPI Cox & Wyman, Reading, Berkshire RG1 8EX

www.simonandschuster.co.uk and www.nick.co.uk

iWanna Stay

Part One

ISPY A
MEAN
TEACHER

CHAPTER 1

Carly Shay and her best friend, Samantha Puckett, headed for their lockers after what seemed like an incredibly long math class.

"Ugh, class was so boring," Sam complained.

"How would you know?" Carly asked. "You were asleep the whole time."

"Then I guess I dreamed it was boring," Sam said.

"Well, your dream came true," Carly answered, wondering how their teacher had managed to be even more boring today than he had been the day before. Seriously, how were they expected to learn anything when teachers droned on and on and on about random, uninteresting stuff?

Freddie Benson, Carly's neighbor, ran up to them carrying a big piece of bright green fabric. "Hey, guess what I got from the audio visual

3

department?" he asked excitedly. He unfolded the fabric. It looked like a giant green tablecloth.

The girls pretended to be as excited as Freddie was.

"Wow!" Carly said.

Sam chimed in with "Cool!"

Freddie was clearly waiting for more enthusiasm.

Carly flipped her long, brown hair over her shoulder. "Awesome!" she added.

"Amazing!" the girls said together.

Then they admitted that they had no idea what was so great about the giant green tablecloth. In fact, Carly thought, it was downright hideous.

"We don't know what that is," Carly admitted.

"Not a clue," Sam added. "And don't care."

"It's called a green screen," Freddie explained.

Carly and Sam eyed each other with confused expressions. A green screen?

"We can use it for special effects on *iCarly*," Freddie told them. "You guys stand in front of it, and I have this software that can make it any kind of background we want."

Now Carly understood. Freddie loved all things high-tech. When Carly first got the idea for a weekly Web show, Freddie had immediately volunteered to be the show's technical producer. It helped that he had all the latest camera equipment and knew how to use it. He was always coming up with ways to make their live Webcast more exciting.

Even the name of the show, *iCarly*, had been Freddie's idea. "i — Internet. Carly — you," he had explained. Carly and Sam had both loved it.

Freddie had all kinds of technical tricks to use. Carly was amazed by how much he knew about that stuff. She was glad her job was to be in front of the camera and not behind it. She didn't think she could keep everything running as smoothly as Freddie did.

Sam was Carly's sidekick on the show. They had been best friends for as long as Carly could remember. Sam was crazy, fun, and unpredictable, but she was also a great friend. And she was hilarious! Carly needed both Freddie and Sam to make the show a success. So far it had been a hit.

Kids were tuning in every week and telling their friends to watch, too.

Now that Carly understood what the giant green tablecloth was for she got excited about it for real. "Oh, so you could make it look like we're in a snowstorm, or standing on the moon or something?" Carly asked.

"Exactly," Freddie told her.

"Can you make it look like I'm standing on your face?" Sam asked.

Carly knew her best friend was only half joking. Sam and Freddie didn't exactly get along. Sam knew exactly how to push Freddie's buttons. And she did — all the time. She could always find new ways to insult Freddie, and Freddie always got mad.

Carly often found herself acting as peacemaker. It could be exhausting, but what else could she do? *iCarly* couldn't run without Freddie. Sam was just as important.

Now Freddie was mad at Sam as usual. "Must you always attack me with words?" he asked.

Sam didn't miss a beat. "What do you want me to use?"

"Aw man —" Freddie's response was cut off when Tareen Johnson ran up waving her cell phone. "Hey, guys!" she said, jumping up and down. She was even more excited than Freddie had been a few moments before.

"Hi, Tareen," Carly said.

Sam grabbed a book out of her locker. "Hey, Tareen."

"You'll never guess who I saw at the Cuddle Fish concert last night," Tareen said, talking super fast.

"Who'd you see at the concert?" Carly asked.

"Our history teacher, Mr. Stern!" Tareen announced. She showed them the screen on her cell phone. "Look, I got a picture of him at the concert last night. Look at it," she demanded. "Look at the phone."

Carly, Sam, and Freddie all looked at the phone.

Tareen didn't get the response she expected. "Are you looking at it?" she asked.

"We're looking," Sam said.

"Yes, we see," Carly and Freddie said together.

"That's Mr. Stern?" Sam asked. All she saw was the back of his head.

Carly was shocked. "Are you sure?" she asked. "Teachers shouldn't go to concerts!"

Freddie looked more closely and noticed something else. "It looks like he's dancing."

"He was!" Tareen assured them. "It was awesome! I still can't believe it, and I'm the one who took the picture with my cell phone." She barely took a breath. "Can you believe Mr. Stern was at the concert? And he was dancing? I mean, what else do you think he gets up to? Can you imagine . . . ?"

Tareen's questions spilled out so quickly that Carly could hardly listen fast enough.

"I can't!" Tareen said, answering herself. "I've got to go."

Carly watched Tareen race down the hall, kids jumping out of her way. All that high energy was exhausting. Carly got tired just watching her. "I like Tareen, but after she talks to me I feel like I need a nap," she said.

"I can't believe Mr. Stern would go to a concert," Sam said, totally amazed.

"Yeah, you don't really think about teachers having lives outside of school," Freddie agreed.

"I always thought they just locked them up in the teachers' lounge at night," Sam joked. The thought of teachers outside their natural habitat was something Sam couldn't handle. Outside of school, Sam didn't want to see any part of them.

The bell rang. The girls closed their lockers and headed toward their next class. Freddie was right behind them.

They could hear one of the teachers in their school — Miss Briggs — coming down the stairs and yelling at everyone in her path. As if her voice wasn't loud and screechy enough on its own, she had gotten a hold of a bullhorn.

"Hey! Get to class!" she said to some guys on the stairs. "You — stop laughing," she said to another. "I said get to class," she said fiercely at someone who wasn't moving quite fast enough for her. "Respect the bullhorn!"

The *iCarly* team watched her chase after some poor kid who had stopped to tie his shoe.

"That Miss Briggs is a joy, isn't she?" Sam asked sarcastically.

Carly rolled her eyes. "I wonder what she does when she's not in school?" Somehow she knew Miss Briggs wasn't attending any Cuddle Fish concerts.

"She probably spits on puppies," Freddie said.

Miss Briggs was still yelling at random kids. "Hey, you, get to class!"

Suddenly, Carly got a brilliant idea. "Hey, that could be a really cool idea for our Web show."

"We use a bullhorn?" Sam asked.

Carly shot her best friend an "are you crazy?" look. "I meant we could do a whole segment on what teachers do when they're not in school," she explained.

Freddie's eyes lit up. "*Niiiiiice*," he said.

Liking Carly and her ideas was the one thing Freddie and Sam agreed upon.

"I love your brain," Sam said.

"My brain says thanks," Carly told her.

The three of them watched Miss Briggs chase some more kids up the stairs. "Come on! Keep going!" she shouted into her bullhorn. "Move!"

"So how do we do this?" Freddie asked.

"We follow Miss Briggs around after school," Carly explained. "You know, with a video camera, and just see what she does."

"And what if she's boring?" Sam asked.

They watched a seventh grader approach the teacher with a sweet smile. "Miss Briggs, I picked you an orange from my mother's tree," he said, handing her the piece of fruit.

Miss Briggs took the orange and slammed it to the floor. "I'm allergic to citrus fruit!" she yelled, stomping on the orange. It splattered all over the kid's sneakers. Then Miss Briggs raised her bull-horn again and screamed in his ear. "Now get to class!"

Carly watched the boy run away. Miss Briggs, boring? That was highly unlikely. "I'm thinking that's not going to happen," she said to her friends.

CHAPTER 2

A few days later, Carly, Sam, and Freddie were hanging out in the *iCarly* studio after school, planning the next Webcast. Carly lived in an old high-rise industrial building in downtown Seattle with her older brother, Spencer. Spencer was an artist and totally cool. When the building had been converted to apartments and artists' lofts, he and Carly had moved in.

Carly's father, a military officer, was stationed on a submarine. So Spencer became Carly's guardian. Some people thought it was strange that a thirteen-year-old girl lived with her twenty-six-year-old brother, but Carly wouldn't have it any other way.

Spencer was definitely offbeat, but part of the fun of living with him was never knowing what new piece of art Carly would come home to — a giant robot made out of soda bottles, a fish-feeding machine, a camcorder transformed into a squirrel. More than that, Spencer was always there for his sister. The two of them looked out for each other.

Spencer had been cool with the idea of Carly and her friends turning the third floor of their loft into a studio where they could do their Webcast. It was a big open space, and they had fixed it up to make it look really great. There was plenty of room for all of Freddie's high-tech equipment, and Spencer's light sculptures made awesome props. There was even a neon *iCarly* sign.

Freddie had rigged up a flat screen TV on a robotic arm. They used it to play back videos their viewers emailed to *iCarly*. He had also created a remote control for sound effects. Handling the remote was Sam's territory. She could push a button to fill the studio with cheers and applause, boos, and even dance music and flashing lights.

Today, Freddie was ready to show them his latest piece of high-tech — or as Sam would say, high-geek — gear.

"Okay, inside this box is a new piece of

technological equipment that's going to amaze you guys," Freddie announced.

"What is it?" Carly said.

"Did you buy yourself a robot girlfriend?" Sam asked with a deadpan expression.

"I don't need a robot girlfriend," Freddie told her. "Twenty years from now, I guarantee you I will be Carly's second husband."

It didn't matter how many times Carly told Freddie she just wanted to be friends, Freddie had a major crush on Carly, and it wasn't going away. Until now, Carly had no idea how far Freddie had taken things in his imagination.

Second husband? She looked at him, her forehead wrinkled in confusion. "What happened to my first husband?" she asked.

"Nothing you can prove," Freddie said firmly.

"Just show us what's in the box before I get bored and leave," Sam said, changing the subject.

"There's nothing boring about being able to tape Miss Briggs with no chance of her catching us," Freddie told her.

Carly's ears perked up. "What'd you get?" she asked.

"A teeny video camera disguised as a piece of pie," Freddie said. He opened a box and pulled out a plastic piece of pie.

Only it wasn't the teeny camera Freddie was expecting. It was huge! The plastic pie — Freddie had ordered cherry — was big enough to feed a giant. The lens on the side of it was giant, too. Giant and obvious. Even the plate the pie was glued to was oversized.

Carly and Sam both cracked up.

"Yeah, who wouldn't that fool?" Sam joked.

Freddie looked at the pie-cam. It wasn't quite what he expected when he ordered it over the Internet. The picture online made it look like a real piece of pie. "It looks real," he said half-heartedly. He wasn't sure if he was trying to convince the girls or himself.

"Yes, a real gigantic piece of plastic pie with a camera lens on the side," Carly said, still laughing.

Sam looked in the box and found a matching

utensil, also humungous. "Look, it comes with a giant fork," she laughed.

Freddie hated being laughed at, especially by Sam. "Give it!" He snatched the fork away from her and held up the pie-cam. "This is a quality piece of spy equipment!" he insisted.

"My aunt Maggie's red wig looks more real than that, and she looks ridiculous," Sam said.

Carly could see how frustrated Freddie was. "I really don't think you're going to fool anyone with that thing," she said gently.

"Oh, you don't?" Freddie asked, ready to prove her wrong. "Where's Spencer?"

"Downstairs with his friend, Connie," Carly said.

Freddie threw his shoulders back and prepared to win this argument. "BRB," he said, giving them the text message initials for "Be Right Back." He headed for the stairs, convinced that he'd fool Spencer and come back with some secret footage.

Spencer was hanging out on the couch in the living room with Connie. Freddie snuck in with his pie-cam and set it on the kitchen counter.

Spencer was trying to talk Connie into something. "C'mon, please?" he asked.

Connie shook her head. "No."

"Pretty please?" Spencer pleaded.

Connie was even firmer this time. "No, Spencer."

But Spencer wasn't about to give up. "Pretty please with sugar on top?" he wheedled.

"I'm diabetic, and I said no," Connie insisted.

"I'll be your best buddy," Spencer said in a singsong voice.

Connie sighed. It was clear that Spencer wasn't going to stop asking. "Oh, all right," she said finally, getting to her feet. She pulled three tennis balls out of her purse and started to juggle — expertly.

Spencer jumped to his feet and did a little happy dance. He never got tired of watching Connie juggle. "Yes! That is — " he was about to say "amazing," but he spotted Freddie watching them and stopped short.

17

Connie stopped juggling.

"Oh, don't mind me," Freddie said, pretending to eat his giant slice of pie with his giant fork. "I'm just a guy having some pie."

Spencer took one look at the pie and knew what it was. "Hey, is that one of those pie-spy video cameras?" he asked.

"No, it is not," Freddie said, pretending to take another bite. The empty fork kind of gave him away.

"Oh, yeah! They were talking about those on the Food Channel," Connie said. "Or was it the Spy Channel?"

Spencer had seen it, too. "You know, I think it was the Spy Channel," he answered.

"I don't know what you're talking about," Freddie told them. "This is just a normal piece of pie that doesn't record anything!"

Spencer wasn't fooled. "But there's a big lens on the side," he pointed out.

"Aw, just forget it!" Freddie said, stomping off. Carly and Sam were right. His pie-cam wasn't going to fool anyone. It was giant all right — a giant waste of money.

CHAPTER 3

The next day, Carly and Freddie were crouched behind a low wall on Miss Briggs's patio, watching her vacuum her carpet.

Freddie's pie-cam sat on the top of the wall. He rested his chin on it and sighed. "Two hours of boring," he said. So far they had watched Miss Briggs read the newspaper, dust, do laundry, wash her kitchen floor, and now, vacuum.

Carly sighed, too. "I think we've learned what teachers do when they're not at school."

"Yep," Freddie agreed. "Nothing interesting enough to put on our Webcast."

"Nope," Carly said with a nod.

"Hey, hey, she's opening her door," Freddie said. He aimed his pie-cam at Miss Briggs.

Carly sat up. Maybe Miss Briggs was going outside to do something interesting. But then she and Freddie watched their teacher pick up a big, black plastic bag and take it outside, closing the apartment door behind her.

"Aww, she's just taking out her trash," Carly said. Her shoulders slumped in disappointment.

Freddie and Carly both stood, ready to give up and go home. Who would have thought that someone so mean in school could be so boring at home? She wasn't fighting with her neighbors, picking on the mailman, or even snapping at the television — all of which they imagined. The only thing she had done was clean her condo.

Carly hadn't thought it was possible to be this bored on a spy mission, but she was — bored out of her mind. It was time to come up with a new idea for this week's *iCarly*.

Freddie picked up his pie-cam, and then noticed something buzzing above his head. "Hey! Go away!" he said, waving his arms. "Get out of here!"

Carly looked up. "It's just a bee," she told him.

"You don't understand!" Freddie said, dodging the bee. "I'm extremely allergic to bees!" He tried to swat it away. "Get out of here, you stupid bee!"

The bee buzzed past Freddie's ear, and then flew toward him again. It did a figure eight around his head.

Freddie was beginning to panic. "I think he wants my pie!" he said.

"That is a stupid bee," Carly said. *Couldn't it see that the pie wasn't real?* she wondered.

Freddie shoved the pie-cam into Carly's hands and jumped back. He fell over the wall and onto Miss Briggs's patio.

The bee followed him, buzzing around his face.

Desperately, Freddie jumped up and pulled on Miss Briggs's sliding glass door. The bee swooped around him, coming closer and closer.

Carly's eyes widened in disbelief when she realized what Freddie was about to do. "Where are you going?" she asked.

Freddie was willing to do anything to avoid getting stung. He didn't think about whose apartment he was about to enter. He just yanked the sliding glass door open, ran into Miss Briggs's home, and closed the door behind him. "I can't get stung!" he yelled through the glass.

"Are you insane?" Carly asked. "Get out of Miss Briggs's apartment! You can't just —"

She was cut off by the bee. It had left the patio and was now buzzing around Carly. She screamed, sure she was about to get stung. "Get away! It's a fake pie!" she told the bee. "Can't you see the big lens on the side?"

The bee zipped past Carly's head. It circled and flew back again, and then again. The last time she was sure she saw the stinger, and it was aimed directly at her nose. She screamed again, dropped the pie-cam, and followed Freddie into Miss Briggs's apartment. She slid the door closed behind her and yelled at the bee one more time. "It's a fake pie!"

Once she was inside, all Carly could think about was getting out again before Miss Briggs came back. She grabbed Freddie by the arm and pulled him toward the door. "C'mon, we can't stay in here! If Miss Briggs catches us we're in big trouble!"

Freddie watched the bee buzz around on the patio. It wasn't giving up! Freddie was convinced that the insect was waiting for him to come outside so that it could sting him.

Why does that bee want to hurt me? Freddie wondered. *What did I ever do to him?*

"Let's go!" Carly urged.

At that moment, Freddie was more afraid of the bee than he was of Miss Briggs. "No!" he said, pulling away from her. "That bee's still out there and by now he knows my pie was fake — he's going to be angrier than ever!"

They heard the sound of a key being inserted into the lock on the front door. It had to be Miss Briggs!

"Here she comes!" Carly whispered, totally panicked.

She and Freddie frantically looked around for a place to hide.

Carly ran one way and Freddie ran the other. They banged into each other and almost knocked each other down.

Carly spotted a door and pointed. "Go in there!" she said.

Together they ran across the room and

through the door. They had found a closet. Luckily, they got the door closed just before Miss Briggs entered her living room. But now they were trapped in Miss Briggs's apartment. There was no way out without the teacher seeing them.

"Now what do we do?" Freddie whispered.

"Shhh!" Carly told him. "I'm thinking."

Freddie started to warm up to the idea of being stuck in a closet with his crush. "You know, this might not be so bad," he said. "Just you and me . . . together . . . alone —"

Carly cut him off with a loud, frustrated whisper. "Okay, we are in a serious situation here."

"Sorry," Freddie said sheepishly.

Carly was still focused on the fact that Miss Briggs would expel them if she found them hiding in her closet. "We cannot let Miss Briggs find us!" she told Freddie.

"Well, maybe we can wait until she goes into another room," Freddie suggested. "Then we can make a run for it."

"Maybe," Carly agreed. "Now *shhhh*." She quietly opened the door and peeked into Miss

Briggs's living room. The teacher was rolling on a big exercise ball, trying to do ab crunches.

Freddie couldn't see over Carly's shoulder. But he heard Miss Briggs's grunting and he saw his friend close the door again with a horrified expression. "What's she doing?" he asked.

Carly shuddered and quietly closed the door again. She shook her head. It was too hideous to describe. "You don't want to know," she warned.

Meanwhile, Spencer was getting his modeling clay out and making sure he had the tools he needed to create a new sculpture. Sam had agreed to come over and help him.

"Hey, thanks for doing this," he said, when Sam rang the doorbell.

"No prob," Sam answered, taking off her jacket.

"How come you're not hanging with Carly and Freddie?" he asked.

"I don't always hang out with them," she told him. Then Sam looked around for a place to perch. Being artistic was something new for Sam, although she knew Carly had helped Spencer a few times. "So how can I help?" she asked.

Spencer pointed to a stool in the kitchen. "Oh, you just sit over there and do nothing," he said.

Sam laughed. "Cool, that sounds easy." She climbed up onto the stool, checked her cell phone, and waited for Spencer to begin.

Spencer looked from the clay to Sam and back to the clay again with a thoughtful expression. For some reason, he wasn't quite seeing the sculpture that wanted to emerge from the clay.

Sam could tell that Spencer wasn't exactly inspired at the moment. Trying to help, she gave him an encouraging smile.

"Yes!" Spencer yelled, giving her a big smile in return. Then he started working on his big lump of clay.

Carly and Freddie were still trapped in the dark closet. Carly opened the door a crack to peek at Miss Briggs. She had finished her crunches and moved on to leg lifts.

"Seventy-seven," the teacher said with a huff. "Seventy-eight. Seventy-nine." It seemed like she would never stop.

Carly turned around and whispered to Freddie. "*Sooo* many leg lifts," she said, wondering how much longer they would be trapped.

A sliver of light came through the crack in the door, and Freddie used it to check out the dark closet. "Hey, I think I found the light switch," he told Carly. "Shut the door."

Carly closed the door and Freddie flicked on the light. He turned around to find himself face-to-face with a life-sized cardboard cutout of the *American Idol* judge, Randy Jackson.

At first Freddie thought Randy was real. He pointed, ready to scream.

Carly threw her hand over Freddie's mouth to keep him quiet while she looked around the closet. "Shhhhhh!" she begged.

Freddie calmed down and Carly slowly removed her hand from his mouth. The closet was completely filled with pictures of Randy Jackson. It was like a shrine to him and to *American Idol*, the television show that gave amateur singers the opportunity to compete for a record contract.

In addition to the life-sized cardboard cutout, Miss Briggs had filled her closet with Randy Jackson posters, magazine pictures of him in fancy frames, T-shirts, bobblehead dolls, mugs, collector plates, and even Randy Jackson food. Miss Briggs was obsessed with the *American Idol* judge!

Carly's jaw dropped. She was completely and totally stunned. Could this be real, or was she not getting enough oxygen? "Freddie?" she asked.

"Yeah?" Freddie answered, equally stunned.

"Am I seeing things or are we surrounded by two thousand Randy Jacksons?" she asked.

Freddie nodded. He couldn't believe his eyes either. "Why does Miss Briggs have all this stuff?"

"I don't know," Carly answered. "I guess if you're going to be obsessed with an *American Idol* judge, you might as well pick one that's firm but fair."

Freddie took a step back and banged into the life-sized Randy Jackson. It spoke!

"Yeah, dawg, you did your thing!"

Freddie froze. Carly jumped. Randy was loud!

"Shhh! You want Miss Briggs to hear us?" Carly said.

"Randy said it, not me!" Freddie told her.

Carly quickly peeked out of the closet door again. Miss Briggs had stopped exercising and seemed to be listening. Carly saw the teacher get to her feet.

"She's coming! Hide!" Carly said, turning out the light.

She and Freddie looked around in the dark, searching for something to crawl behind. They both ended up crouched behind the life-sized Randy Jackson.

One of them banged into Randy's voice recorder again. Randy Jackson's voice filled the closet. "That was hot, yo!"

"Aw, please be quiet, Randy Jackson," Carly pleaded in a small voice.

She couldn't say anything more. Miss Briggs had opened the closet door and turned on the light. Any sound or movement would give the two spies away.

CHAPTER 4

Miss Briggs turned on the light in her Randy Jackson closet and happily gazed at all the pictures she had collected of the *American Idol* judge.

"Good afternoon, Randy Jackson," Miss Briggs said with a huge smile on her face. "Oh, you are looking spiffy today," she said in a sweet voice. "Now, is there something you'd like to say to me?" She pretended to tickle Randy and then pushed one of the buttons on his shirt.

"Yeah, we got us a hot one tonight, baby!" Randy said.

Miss Briggs giggled. "Oh, R.J.," she said flirtatiously.

Was Miss Briggs actually giggling and acting like a little kid with a crush? A crush on a cardboard man? Gross!

Carly and Freddie had to work hard not to laugh.

Across town, Sam was already bored. She couldn't see Spencer's sculpture, but it sounded like he was working hard.

"So this is seriously the first time you've ever helped with a sculpture?" Spencer asked.

"First time," Sam told him. But she had to admit she didn't actually feel like she was doing anything. "How am I doing?"

"Good!" Spencer exclaimed. Sam had actually managed to sit quietly for all that time. He was impressed.

Sam couldn't wait to see what Spencer was creating. "Can I sneak a peek?"

"Yeah, sure. Why not?" Spencer said. He put down his sculpting tools and stepped back.

Sam ran over to look at his sculpture. She knew Spencer's art could be abstract and modern, so she was prepared to find something that didn't look like anything normal. But what she found was really . . . odd. She looked at the sculpture and then at Spencer.

Spencer gave her a small grin and waited to hear what she had to say.

"Spencer?" Sam asked.

"Mmm?" Spencer said.

Sam stated the obvious. "That's a fish," Sam said.

"Yeah, a tuna!" Spencer said happily. "Or, I suppose you could argue that it's a trout." Spencer pointed to the fish's mouth. "You know, because of the way his lips curl up right here —"

Sam cut him off. She didn't really want to hear about fish mouths after sitting absolutely still for three hours. Did she really get a backache and a stiff neck so that Spencer could make a red and yellow fish with blue stripes? "This is what you've been doing for the past three hours?"

"Well," Spencer explained. "I started thinking about aquariums and" — he pointed at the fish — "he happened."

Sam eyed him quizzically. "Then why am I still here?" she asked him. "I thought I was supposed to help."

"I get lonely," Spencer admitted in a small voice.

Sam shook her head. She was ready to yell at him, but her cell phone rang. "What?" she said into the phone.

It was Carly, calling from Miss Briggs's closet. Miss Briggs had had a long, giggly talk with Randy, and then left the *American Idol* judge alone while she cleaned some more. Carly took advantage of the teacher's absence to call for help.

"Sam, listen," Carly whispered. "Freddie and I are stuck. We're hiding in a closet in Miss Briggs's apartment!"

Sam's frustration with Spencer and his fish sculpture suddenly lifted. She even forgot about her stiff neck. This was too funny! "Really? That's some nutty stuff."

"Can you just get over here?" Carly asked.

"On my way," Sam assured her.

Carly hung up and turned to Freddie. "Sam's on her way."

Freddie had a mouthful of a Randy Jackson cereal. Carly snatched the box from him. "And will you quit eating the Randy-Yo's!" she said.

Carly was hungry, too. They'd been stuck in here for hours! She watched Freddie swallow his last bite and then grabbed a handful of Randy-Yo's herself. The yo's didn't actually taste that bad. *But how long had they been sitting in the closet?* she wondered.

Sam tiptoed through the bushes behind Miss Briggs's apartment. She heard an awful sound coming from inside. The teacher must have found her friends!

"No way!" Sam said to herself. "She's hurting Carly and Freddie!" She stumbled across the pie-cam Carly had dropped when she was running away from the bee. Sam picked it up and noticed again how fake it looked.

Sam crouched behind the patio wall and peered through the sliding glass doors. Miss Briggs was marching up and down in front of her couch, playing the bagpipes.

"Bagpipes?" Sam said.

Meanwhile, Carly and Freddie were crouched in the closet with their hands over their ears. They had been listening to Miss Briggs play the bagpipes for an hour. It was definitely not Carly and Freddie's idea of great music!

"This is torture," Carly said. Her cell phone vibrated.

"Sam?" Freddie asked.

Carly checked her caller ID. "Yeah," she told him. "Where are you?" she whispered into the phone.

"I'm right outside on the patio," Sam told her. "What's the plan, man?"

Carly had been thinking about this ever since she called Sam, and she had come up with an idea. Sam would capture Miss Briggs's attention so that Carly and Freddie could sneak out of the apartment without being seen — and punished.

"Okay, you call Miss Briggs," Carly said. "Then keep her distracted on the phone while Freddie and I sneak out the front door."

Sam nodded. "One distraction coming up. Give me sixty seconds, then go for the door."

"See you on the outside," Carly said, hanging up.

Freddie took one last handful of Randy-Yo's, and the two of them got to their feet.

Miss Briggs was still huffing and puffing into her bagpipes when the phone rang a minute later. She set them down and answered.

"Briggs," she barked into the phone.

Sam hid behind a plant on the patio and watched the teacher through the glass doors. She deepened her voice. "Hello, ma'am," she said into the phone. "Have you purchased any suspicious milk lately?"

"Suspicious milk?" Miss Briggs asked. She sounded suspicious herself. "Who is this?" she demanded.

Sam did some quick thinking. "Uh, this is Agent McMuffen with the, uh, Federal Bureau of Milk."

"The FBM?" Miss Briggs asked.

"Uh, sure," Sam said, wondering if there really was such a thing. "See, there have been some reports of counterfeit milk and other dairy products in the Seattle area."

Miss Briggs not only believed the caller, she even got a little scared about the dairy products she had been eating. "Oh, no! I just bought a tub of zingleberry yogurt yesterday," Miss Briggs said.

"It's okay, ma'am," Sam assured her. She relied

on all the cop shows she had seen to come up with her instructions. "Just remain calm and proceed to your refrigerator."

"Of course," Miss Briggs said, hurrying to her refrigerator. She opened the door and looked inside.

Carly and Freddie had the perfect opportunity to slip out unnoticed. Sam couldn't believe her teacher was actually falling for something as crazy as counterfeit milk. All it took was a deep voice and a fake government agency to fool her. "Ha," Sam muttered to herself, shaking her head. Then she winced. Her mouth was way too close to the phone when she said that.

Miss Briggs looked up. Had she heard something?

CHAPTER 5

Inside the closet, Freddie nervously danced from foot to foot while Carly watched the clock on her cell phone.

"It's been sixty seconds." Carly said. "Let's make our move and get out of here."

Freddie stopped her. "Wait." He grabbed something off a shelf and shoved it into his pocket. "Okay, ready," he said.

"What did you put in your pocket?" Carly asked. It was one thing to spy on Miss Briggs, it was another to steal from her. Besides, what could Freddie possibly want from this bizarre Randy Jackson closet?

Freddie sheepishly pulled a bottle out of his pocket.

Carly took it from him. "Randy Jackson cologne?" she asked. "Why do you want this?"

"Because," Freddie said, pointing to the label

on the front. He imitated Randy Jackson's voice and read, "'It smells tight, dawg.'"

Miss Briggs was still on the phone with Sam. "The milk smells just fine to me," she said. "Are you sure there's a dairy problem?" she asked.

Sam got worried. What if Miss Briggs hung up before her friends were safely out of the apartment. "You're losing precious time!" she said urgently.

"I already checked my milk and my tub of yogurt," Miss Briggs said firmly. She was beginning to lose her patience with the FBM agent.

Sam was getting desperate. Miss Briggs sounded like she was ready to hang up and there was still no sign of Carly and Freddie. She peered through the glass patio doors.

She needed Miss Briggs to look in the fridge again. Sam could see right inside from her perch behind the plant. "Yeah, but you'd better inspect that cottage cheese on the top shelf," she said.

"All right," Miss Briggs said, turning back to the refrigerator. "But I don't see why —" She stopped short. Top shelf? "How did you know my cottage cheese was on the top shelf?" she demanded.

Sam's eyes widened. What had she done? She did her best to recover and gain control. "Because I'm a professional, ma'am," she said in her deep voice.

Miss Briggs looked around. How did her caller know she had cottage cheese on the top shelf of her refrigerator? She realized that someone on the patio would be able to see inside. She walked over toward the doors.

Sam saw Miss Briggs bearing down on her and panicked. "Don't go near your patio door!" she said into the phone. She babbled the first thing that came to mind. "There's a dairy monster on the loose and you don't want to see what —"

Miss Briggs slid open her patio door and spotted Sam crouched behind a plant. "Busted! Now get inside," the teacher ordered.

Busted was right, Sam thought. But maybe she could still save her friends by making sure Miss Briggs stayed focused on her and not whatever was going on behind her. "I . . . I can explain," Sam stammered, getting to her feet.

"I'm sure you can," Miss Briggs said sarcastically. Clearly, she didn't believe her. At school, Sam was always getting called to the principal's office for pulling one crazy stunt or another.

"I can," Sam said. "See I'm doing a school project on . . ." She watched Carly open the closet door and step into the living room, ". . . on how ladies react when they think their dairy products are —"

Suddenly there was a loud crash and the sound of bagpipes squealing. Freddie had tripped over Miss Briggs's instrument, giving them away.

"Freddie!" Carly said in a loud whisper.

But it was too late. Miss Briggs turned around and saw the two of them creeping across her living room and toward her front door.

Carly and Freddie looked at each other, totally panicked. Then they both got the same idea. Carly threw her arms wide open. Freddie did the same. "Surprise!" they shouted together.

"Yeah! Happy Birthday, Miss Briggs!" Sam said, picking up on her friends' plan.

"Let's sing her a birthday song!" Carly suggested brightly.

Sam ran over to stand with Carly and Freddie. All together, the *iCarly* team members sang, "For she's a jolly good fellow. For she's a jolly good fellow —"

Miss Briggs cut them off with a scream. "It's not my birthday!"

"Whoops, then we'd better go," Carly said. "C'mon, kids."

They headed for the front door. Had Miss Briggs fallen for their birthday scheme?

Carly quickly learned that the teacher hadn't fallen for anything.

"Stop!" Miss Briggs barked.

Carly, Sam, and Freddie turned to find Miss Briggs glaring at them.

Okay, so the birthday thing hadn't worked, but it gave Sam another idea. Holidays were always a good reason to visit people. "Happy . . . Hanukkah?" she said hopefully.

Miss Briggs's glare only got more angry and more intense.

Carly tried, too. "Kwanzaa?" she asked in a

small voice, still searching for a holiday they might pretend to celebrate.

Miss Briggs's expression made it clear — she wasn't buying it. She was too angry to speak. She pointed to the couch, indicating that she wanted the three of them to sit down and be quiet. They sat silently and miserably, afraid to move, while the teacher examined her bagpipes.

Carly gave Freddie a nudge and nodded in Miss Briggs's direction. She had seen Miss Briggs angry before. In fact, angry was Miss Briggs's normal everyday mood. But Carly had never seen her quite this upset. Freddie had to say something about stepping on the instrument.

"I'm sorry I tripped on your bagpipes," Freddie said nervously.

"Are they okay?" Carly asked.

"No," Miss Briggs barked, outraged. "He dented my blow stick and punctured my squeeze bag!"

"Freddie will pay to have your bagpipes fixed," Sam said generously.

Now Freddie was the one glaring — at Sam. She was spending money he didn't have, and he still had to pay for the pie-cam.

Miss Briggs wasn't impressed with Sam's generosity either, but for different reasons. "And you think that'll get the three of you out of trouble?" she asked.

"Well, we were kind of hoping," Carly said with a friendly little laugh.

Miss Briggs responded with a menacing chuckle. "I don't think so." She stood and paced while she listed all of the ways the three of them had broken the rules that day. "Breaking into a teacher's home, damaging property, impersonating a dairy agent." She stopped pacing and got very serious. "I could have you expelled. I might even call the police," she threatened.

Sam proposed another solution. "Or you could just let us run away while you angrily shake your fist in the air and scream" — she raised her fist and made her voice sound like a very old lady's — "'you rotten kids!'"

Miss Briggs put her hands on her hips and glared at Sam.

Carly stood, realizing that Sam was about to get them into even more trouble. "Look, Miss

Briggs," she said seriously. "We never meant to sneak into your house."

"Then explain why you did," the teacher demanded.

Carly realized she was going to have to tell the truth to avoid getting expelled, or worse, arrested. "We were taping you for our Web show, to sort of see what teachers are like when they're not in school," she explained.

"Ah, your little Web show, *iCarly*," Miss Briggs said, mocking her. "I've seen it. It's nothing more than mucus in the nose of the digital age."

Mucus in the nose of the digital age? Huh?

Carly had to think about that for a second. Then she realized what Miss Briggs was really saying. "Did she just call our show a booger?" Carly asked her friends.

"*iCarly*'s great," Freddie said defensively. "Thousands of people watch it every week."

"Thousands?" Miss Briggs asked, sounding interested.

"That's a pretty big booger," Sam told her.

Miss Briggs was silent for a moment, thinking. "Well, since you're so interested in showing your viewers what teachers do outside of school," she said finally, "I think I have a solution that will benefit us all."

Uh-oh. Carly did not trust the look that had crept across Miss Briggs's face. She could tell they would not enjoy this. "What solution?" she asked reluctantly.

"I won't suspend you from school, or call the police, if you let me perform an original bagpipe song on your Web show," Miss Briggs said.

"You want to be on *iCarly*?" Freddie asked in disbelief. Who wanted to see Miss Briggs play her bagpipes? Their viewers would hate every second of that. *iCarly*'s audience would plummet from the thousands to the hundreds and then down to the tens. It would be awful!

Sam felt the same way. "Just call the cops on us," she said.

"Sam!" Carly said, shushing her. "Why would you even want to be on our show?" she asked Miss Briggs.

"Because I see this as a great opportunity,"

Miss Briggs said. "To show the world some culture. To teach young people about fine music."

"Don't do it, Carls," Sam urged. "She's not even playing yet and I'm already bored out of my mind."

Carly agreed. Bagpipes on *iCarly* would be a complete disaster, but she also didn't want to get suspended. And she really didn't want to go to jail. She had to find a way to talk Miss Briggs out of this! "Look, Miss Briggs —"

But Miss Briggs had made up her mind, and she wouldn't take no for an answer. "Put me on your Webcast or I will have you suspended for breaking into my house, and I'll file a report with the Seattle police department." She pointed at them, one at a time. "Your choice."

Carly, Sam, and Freddie realized that they had no real choice. They had to say yes, but would the hard work they had done on their show be for nothing? Would they lose all their viewers? What if it meant the end of *iCarly*?

CHAPTER 6

A few days later, Miss Briggs showed up for the newest, and possibly last, installment of *iCarly*. She waited offstage with her bagpipes and some sheet music.

Freddie pointed his camera at Carly and Sam, and counted down the seconds until they went live. "In five, four, three, two . . ." Instead of saying one, as always, he pointed to the girls.

"Hey there. Welcome to *iCarly*," Carly said into the camera. She was a lot less enthusiastic than she usually was when she greeted her live viewers.

Sam was even more unenthusiastic. "I'm Sam," she said quietly.

"I'm Carly," Carly added.

Sam couldn't even bring herself to say anything good about that night's show. "Blah blah," she said.

48

Carly agreed. "Blah blah."

Miss Briggs peered at them from backstage. "Hey, just read the introduction I gave you!" she ordered in a loud whisper.

Carly and Sam exchanged looks. They had been dreading this moment for days, and now it was upon them. It was even worse than they imagined it would be.

Carly read from the paper Miss Briggs had given her. "Tonight on *iCarly*, instead of the worthless trash we usually do here, please prepare to enjoy some fine music, played on the bagpipes by Miss Francine Briggs."

Sam pressed a button on her remote control and filled the loft with the sound of boos and raspberries. "Oops, wrong button," she said sarcastically.

"Give me that," Carly said, taking the remote from Sam. She read the rest of the introduction. "And now, here she is, playing an original song she composed herself, called 'Haggis and Moonlight.'" Carly could hardly keep the dread out of her voice as she finished. "Please welcome the lovely and talented Miss Francine Briggs."

She and Sam applauded halfheartedly and Miss Briggs took the stage. She was dressed in Scottish plaid, complete with a kilt, a sash, and a hat with a red pompom.

"Thank you," Miss Briggs said, taking a stool. "And now, for some real, enriching entertainment."

Enriching? *Our audience wants to be entertained, not enriched*, Carly thought.

Carly and Sam joined Freddie at his tech station. He had put the camera on a tripod so that he could keep an eye on everything.

Sam winced as Miss Briggs began huffing and puffing into her blow stick. The sound the teacher made was a cross between a high-pitched pig's squeal and car brakes screeching. "This is so horrible," she said.

Carly tried to look on the bright side. "Well, maybe we don't have a big audience tonight."

Freddie checked their stats on his laptop. "Sorry, look," he said, pointing to his laptop screen.

"Whoa! All those people are streaming us right now?" Carly asked.

Freddie nodded. "Biggest audience we've ever had," he said grimly.

"Yeah, and they all want us to be out there doing something funny," Sam said. She shook her head. Watching Miss Briggs torture their audience was terrible. Miss Briggs looked happier than Sam had ever seen her. It was downright wrong!

"Hey, hey, look at that," Freddie said, pointing to his laptop. The number of viewers was falling fast.

"Why's the number dropping?" Carly asked.

"Because people are turning us off," Freddie told her. "We've lost over ten percent of our viewers in less than two minutes!"

"This is a disaster!" Sam said. "Do you know how hard we worked to get that audience?"

Freddie shook his head in defeat. "And Briggs is going to ruin it in one night!" He looked at his screen again. The number had dropped even further. "Look, already, twenty percent of our audience — gone."

The number of viewers kept falling while Miss

Briggs puffed her way through the song. It seemed endless.

"How long is this song?" Sam asked.

Carly checked the clock. "I don't even think it's half over," she moaned.

"Well, we've lost over half our viewers," Freddie said.

"We've got to do something," Sam said.

Carly agreed. She desperately tried to think of something that would save them — and save *iCarly*. She drew a blank, just for a second, and then she had it. A brilliant idea. She opened the door and pulled her friends out into the hall, away from Miss Briggs and her squealing bagpipes.

Carly's face was lit up with excitement.

"What?" Sam asked.

"The green screen!" she said.

"What about the green screen?" Freddie asked.

"Do you have it set up?" Carly asked.

"Yeah, but I haven't tried it yet," Freddie said. "I was going to test it this week and —"

"What?" Sam asked.

"Test it now," Carly said, firmly.

Freddie could tell Carly meant business. "Or I'll test it now," he agreed quickly.

"He'll test it now," Sam assured her.

The three of them went back into the studio. Miss Briggs was still playing the never-ending song.

Carly nodded at Freddie and he pressed a button on his control panel. A red light blinked on and the green screen slowly appeared behind Miss Briggs. She was too into her bagpipes to even notice.

Thumbnail pictures of video clips were displayed on Freddie's laptop. Carly and Sam looked them over, and Carly pointed to one.

Freddie nodded again and hit Play. A video of a chimpanzee popped up behind Miss Briggs. It looked like it was trying to figure out what she was holding.

Carly and Sam tried not to crack up. Carly hit another button and suddenly Miss Briggs seemed to be surrounded by a man chomping on an ear of corn. He chewed with his mouth open, and there were little niblets of corn dangling from his lips. It looked so real, Carly was tempted to reach out and brush the corn niblets off of Miss Briggs's hat!

Sam started to laugh, setting off Carly and Freddie. Miss Briggs glanced at them. The three of them quickly stopped giggling and tried to look knowing and cultured — as if they were actually appreciating Miss Briggs's music. They gave the teacher the thumbs-up. Miss Briggs grinned at them over her bagpipes. She totally believed they were enjoying her song.

For the rest of Miss Briggs's song, they played one bizarre video after another behind her — an elephant and a rhinoceros at a watering hole, a man eating a cabbage, a doll. It was hilarious! And Miss Briggs was totally unaware of the changing background.

Freddie pointed to his laptop again. "Hey, we're getting the audience back," he said in a whisper.

Sam watched the number go up. "Yeah!"

"Awesome," Carly said, giving Freddie and Sam fist bumps.

A rabbit's nose was wiggling behind Miss Briggs when she finally finished her song. The bunny seemed to be trying to eat the red pompom on Miss Briggs's hat.

"Thank you," Miss Briggs said formally into the camera.

Carly and Sam ran over and stood on either side of her.

"Awww, your song's over?" Sam asked.

"Do another one!" Carly said, encouraging the teacher with applause. Now that the green screen was up, Miss Briggs's bagpipes had gone from horrible to hilarious! One more song and they would have the entire audience back.

"Yeah, c'mon, Miss Briggs," Freddie pleaded, clapping along with Carly.

The teacher was incredibly flattered. She had known that once the kids heard her bagpipes they would learn to appreciate the fine music they created. But this reaction was even better than she had anticipated. "All right," she said happily.

Carly and Sam joined Freddie at his control panel while Miss Briggs set up the music for her second song. They selected a new green screen video just as Miss Briggs starting huffing her way through song number two. The rabbit was replaced by cabbage-eating man again, and then by a close-up of a giant, black spider. The *iCarly* team stood back and watched the number of viewers shoot sky-high!

The next day at school, Carly, Sam, and Freddie stood by their lockers and got ready for another day of classes. The halls were crowded with kids comparing homework notes and getting their books from their lockers while they waited for the first bell to ring.

Miss Briggs barreled in as she always did, ready to yell at anyone careless enough to get in her way.

One of *iCarly's* viewers spotted her. "Hey, there's Miss Briggs!" he said.

Everyone who had watched the show, which was basically every kid in the whole school, burst into applause and cheers. Watching Miss Briggs huff and puff on those bagpipes, with no idea what was going on behind her, had been hilarious.

"Why, thank you. Thank you all," Miss Briggs

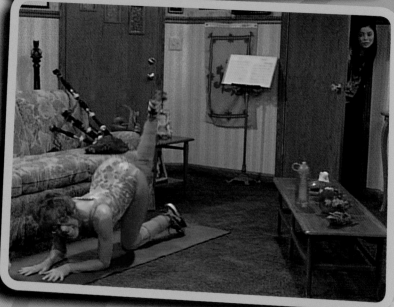

said, taking a bow. She spotted Carly and Sam and walked over to them. "You see? That silly comedy you girls do is no match for my true musical artistry."

Sam nodded solemnly, trying not to burst out laughing. "You are so right," she said seriously.

"Thank you for teaching us that important lesson," Carly added. She bit her lips to keep from totally cracking up.

"Certainly," Miss Briggs said with a satisfied nod. She started to walk away, but she stopped short and started sniffing the air. "Freddie." She came closer and gave him a big sniff. "You smell delightful."

"Thanks, Miss Briggs," Freddie answered with a smile.

The teacher started to walk away again, shooting warm looks at Freddie over her shoulder.

As soon as she was far enough away not to hear, Carly turned to Freddie. "The Randy Jackson cologne?" she asked.

Freddie nodded and pulled the bottle out of his pocket. In all the confusion at Miss Briggs's apartment, he had forgotten to put it back. He smiled at

Carly and read the label, imitating the *American Idol* judge. "It smells tight, dawg," he said.

Carly shook her head with a laugh and headed to class. Freddie smelling like Randy Jackson was a small price to pay after the adventure they had had that week, but she could only imagine how much heckling Sam would be doing if Freddie kept calling everyone "dawg."

Part Two

IWANNA
STAY WITH
SPENCER

CHAPTER 1

Carly and Sam were in the studio getting ready for their next *iCarly* Webcast. The team had a really cool show planned, and they couldn't wait to get started.

Freddie worked his control panel and then picked up his camera. He aimed it at Carly and Sam, and counted down until they were live. "In five, four, three, two . . ." he said. On one, he pointed at the girls, giving them their cue to begin.

"Hey! Welcome to *iCarly*," Carly said into the camera.

"You know who we are," Sam added.

Carly furrowed her brow, as if she was confused. "You don't know?" she asked the audience. "Okay then." She leaned forward so that her face filled the lens and then said in a big voice, "I'm Carly!"

Sam leaned in next to her. "I'm Sam!"

"Now you know!" they sang together.

They jumped back to their normal positions.

"So guess what?" Sam asked their viewers.

"We've been watching some action movies," Carly told them.

Sam shadowboxed the air in front of her. *Pow! Pow! Pow!* "We love watching people fight," she joked.

"Even though we know the punches aren't really real," Carly added.

Sam nodded in agreement. "The actors just swing and miss, but they play a sound effect."

Carly smiled at the camera, and then turned to Sam. "Like this!" she said, swinging her fist toward her friend.

From Freddie's camera angle, it looked like Carly clocked Sam right in the face. There was a loud smacking sound effect, like a fist connecting with skin, and then a heavy thud as Sam hit the floor.

Freddie grinned behind the camera. He kind of enjoyed watching Sam get fake-punched.

"Looked like I punched her, right?" Carly asked.

Sam stood up slowly. She held her face and groaned as if she was in pain. There was blood smeared over her upper lip.

"Oh my gosh!" Carly gasped. "Are you okay?" Had she really punched Sam by accident? That's what it looked like.

"I . . . I think so," Sam said weakly. Then she turned to the camera with a big smile and held up a makeup tube. "Because they also use fake blood!"

"Gotcha!" The girls yelled into the camera with a laugh.

Sam wiped her lip with a towel. "And now moving on," she said.

Carly introduced the next segment. They always invited their viewers to send in videos of themselves doing wacky things to the *iCarly* Website Freddie had created. Every week Carly, Freddie, and Sam picked the funniest ones to air on *iCarly.*

"Last week, one of our viewers submitted an

awesome video clip to us right here at iCarly-dot-com," Carly said.

"It's from Keri Mackler of Providence, Rhode Island," Sam added. "This girl can wail!"

"She's a singer," Carly explained. She turned to Freddie. "Freddie, play Keri's video clip."

Freddie pressed a button on the control panel he wore on his belt. "Playback," he said.

A video began to play on the flat screen TV monitor in the studio. At the same time it was streaming onto the audience's laptops, Carly and Sam watched it along with their viewers.

Keri waived at the camera. "Hi, Carly. Hey, Sam. I love your Web show," she said. "Okay, check this out." Keri put a crystal glass down on a table and then stood behind it. "This is one of my mom's really good glasses. Now watch."

Keri took a breath and then sang a high note — an incredibly, amazingly high note! She held it for about four seconds, and then the glass shattered into a million pieces. Keri had actually broken the glass with her voice! Luckily, she had also covered her face with her hands first so that the flying glass wouldn't hurt her.

Freddie turned off the video and focused his camera on the girls again.

"Nice," Sam exclaimed.

"Did you see that?" Carly said into the camera.

"Why can't she sing that note next to our English teacher's head?" Sam joked.

The show seemed to fly by. Carly and Sam introduced a few more video clips, performed in a comedy sketch, and Sam and Freddie got into a little argument — something their viewers had come to expect and enjoy. Suddenly it was time to bring the show to a close.

"All right, now to finish off tonight's Webcast," Carly said into the camera, "my brother, Spencer . . ."

"An amazing artist," Sam interjected.

". . . is going to show you his latest sculpture," Carly finished.

Sam hadn't seen it yet — none of them had — but she was sure it was great. "It's his coolest one ever," she said.

"So hit the applause button!" Carly told her. Then she turned to the camera. "And say hello to my big brother, Spencer!"

Sam filled the studio with the sound of cheers and applause.

Freddie focused his camera lens on the elevator that ran from the kitchen to the loft's third floor. Spencer knew how to make an entrance. A bell rang and the elevator doors opened. Spencer stood in a strong man's pose with his back to the camera. He turned around and jogged into the studio.

"Yo-yo-dee-yo!" Spencer said into the camera. He stopped next to a large object covered in a white sheet.

"Tell the *iCarly* viewers about your latest masterpiece," Sam said. She knew it wasn't the fish she had spent three hours "helping" create last week. It was too big for that.

"Okay," Spencer said into the camera. Ideas often came to him in a roundabout way, so the viewers were in for an equally roundabout story. "So the other night I'm watching this TV show about building houses, right? And this one guy asked this other guy which he liked better: a nail gun or a hammer. And the guy goes, 'Personally,

I'm a fan of hammers.' And when he said that, it inspired me to build this. . . ."

Spencer pulled the sheet off his sculpture with a flourish. A bright red disk sat on the top of a wooden pole with eight different kinds of hammers attached to the outer edges of the disk.

"A fan of hammers!" Spencer explained, pointing out that the hammers were, in fact, fan blades. He waited for applause to fill the studio. It didn't. "Sam, hit the button," Spencer said.

Sam hit the applause button.

"Thank you!" Spencer said, taking a bow. "I understand your excitement! Hey, check this out — it actually works." He yanked a cord to start the fan's engine and it turned over like a lawn-mower engine, but it didn't catch. He yanked the cord two more times and stepped away as the motor started to rumble, making the fan spin. Soon all they saw was a swirl of hammers. The fan was moving too fast to make out one hammer at a time.

"All right!" Carly said, clapping.

Sam clapped too. "*Fan*-tastic," she joked.

The fan was spinning so fast it started to wobble. Smoke came out of the engine mounted to the back.

"Is it supposed to do that?" Sam asked.

"No, not really, no," Spencer admitted. He tried to turn the fan off, but it was spinning so fast he couldn't get close to it without getting hammered on his hand. It spun faster and faster, and wobbled even more. Then he heard a *ping*, and realized that the hammers could come loose.

"Hit the floor!" Spencer yelled, diving face-first onto a rug.

Carly's eyes widened with fear and she froze for a second. She ducked just as a hammer came flying through the air. It smashed into the wall right where Carly had been standing a second earlier. The fan sputtered and died.

Carly jumped to her feet. She looked at the hammer — completely embedded in the wall — and then at her brother. She was too stunned to speak.

Spencer looked around sheepishly. "It needs to be adjusted," he said in a small voice.

Somehow, Carly and Sam were able to bring the show to a shaky close, relieved and exhausted by Carly's near miss.

CHAPTER 2

The next day after school, Carly, Sam, and Freddie were sprawled on the couch in the loft, eating popcorn and watching television. The doorbell rang.

"I got it," Spencer said from the kitchen.

"If it's Freddie's mom, don't open the door," Sam told him.

Freddie got defensive. "Hey, my mom happens to be —" Then Freddie thought about how over-protective his mom could be. If she came over she'd probably embarrass him in front of Carly. She was always treating him like a baby in front of his friends. "Yeah, don't," he said.

Spencer laughed and opened the door. It wasn't Mrs. Benson. "Granddad!" Spencer said, totally surprised.

"Spencer," Mr. Shay said, giving him a warm handshake.

Carly jumped up. "Granddad!" she said, running over to give him a big hug.

"Carly!" he said. "How's my little gumdrop?"

"Awesome!" Carly told him. "Did you see my Web show last night?"

"Yes, I did and you were adorable," he told her.

"Thanks! So, what are you doing here in Seattle?" Carly asked.

"Why didn't you tell us you were coming?" Spencer said.

"What, a man can't drive ninety minutes to surprise his favorite grandkids?" Mr. Shay asked, pulling them both in for a hug.

Sam noticed how happy they all were to see each other. "How come my grandfather just sleeps and burps?" she asked Freddie.

"Because he's related to you!" Freddie told her.

Sam knew how to handle Freddie's insults. Unlike Freddie, she didn't get mad. She got even. She grabbed a piece of popcorn and shoved it up Freddie's nose.

Carly chose that moment to turn to her friends.

"Oh, you remember Freddie," she said to her grandfather.

Freddie quickly pulled the popcorn out of his nose and waved at Carly's grandfather.

"Of course," Mr. Shay said with a nod. "He lives across the hall."

"And I think you met Sam the last time you were here," Carly said.

Sam kept her eyes on the popcorn, hoping Mr. Shay wouldn't remember.

He did.

"Yes, she borrowed ten dollars from me and then ate my sandwich," Mr. Shay said in a less-than-friendly voice, but then he smiled at her. "How are you, Sam?"

Carly nodded. That was Sam all right. You had to love a girl who was always hungry. Most people learned pretty quickly not to turn their backs on Sam when food was around.

"Nice to see you again," Sam said, wondering if he would ask for his ten dollars back.

But instead he focused on Carly again. "Oh, Carly, I've got a little present for you," Mr. Shay said. He reached into his pocket and handed Carly an envelope.

"Really?" Carly said, opening the envelope. "Oh! A gift card for Groovy Smoothie! Thanks!"

"How much?" Sam asked, peering over Carly's shoulder.

"Sam!" Carly said, scolding her friend. What a rude question!

But Mr. Shay thought Sam was funny. "Thirty bucks," he said with a chuckle.

"Good man," Sam told him. She turned to Carly and Freddie. "Let's go spend that bad boy."

"I can't now," Carly told her. "My granddad just got here."

"Go have fun," Mr. Shay said. "I'm in town a few days."

"Okay!" Carly said with a smile.

"Smooth-eeee," Sam chanted, grabbing her jacket. "Smooth-eeee!"

Freddie slipped his jacket on, too, and followed the girls into the hall.

Spencer watched them leave. "Bring me back a Blueberry Banana Blitz?" he asked.

"Sure," Carly said over her shoulder. "Be back whenever."

"See you whenever," Spencer answered. He turned to his grandfather. "I used to always get the Strawberry Splat but then I tried the Blueberry Banana Blitz —"

Mr. Shay watched Carly and her friends run down the hall. As soon as the elevator doors closed behind his granddaughter and her friends, he slammed the apartment door shut, cutting off Spencer's smoothie explanation. "Are you out of your mind?" Mr. Shay yelled.

Spencer was confused. Why was his grandfather yelling all of a sudden? All he did was ask for a smoothie. "I should have gotten the Strawberry Splat?" he asked.

"I'm talking about your little stunt on Carly's Webcast," Mr. Shay said.

Spencer nodded. It had been pretty scary. "Oh, the fan of hammers," he said.

"You nearly took Carly's head off!" Mr. Shay shouted. "It was incredibly irresponsible."

74

"It was an accident," Spencer said defensively. "And I am *very* responsible."

"Oh, ya think?" Mr. Shay asked sarcastically. "A responsible guardian tells a thirteen-year-old girl she can just come home *whenever*?"

That wasn't a fair example, Spencer thought. He knew exactly where Carly was and who she was with. "She just went across the street," Spencer explained. "And she's with two friends, and she has her cell phone with her at all times."

Mr. Shay wasn't listening. He had already made up his mind about Spencer. "You know, I was not happy when you dropped out of law school to become an artist . . ."

That wasn't exactly news. His granddad had made his opinion very clear at the time — over and over again. Now it was Spencer's turn to be sarcastic. "Wow, really?" he said.

Mr. Shay shook his head in frustration. Unlike art, law was a serious career, and Spencer was certainly smart enough to excel at it. But he believed his grandson had thrown away his chance. "You could've been a fantastic lawyer," Mr. Shay said.

Spencer sighed. This was an old argument and he didn't really want to have it again. Why couldn't his grandfather understand that he was an artist, not a lawyer? Spencer had no regrets. "I didn't want to be a lawyer," he said.

"Why not?" Mr. Shay demanded.

Spencer thought lawyers were all buttoned-up. They had no creative freedom. There was no room in their lives for fun or silliness. To demonstrate his point, he decided to do something incredibly silly.

"Because lawyers can't do this!" Spencer pulled up his shirt and started rubbing circles on his belly while he made loud siren noises.

Mr. Shay watched him in shocked disbelief and then shook his head sadly. "You had such a bright future."

Spencer popped his ear buds in and turned his music player on. "I'm sorry, can't hear you. I'm rocking out!" he yelled. He danced around the apartment, making sure to keep his back to Mr. Shay. He sang along with the music and pretended to ignore his grandfather.

Mr. Shay matched him step for step, ranting to Spencer's back about the crazy artist life he had chosen. "You could've been a brilliant lawyer, that's all I'm trying to say."

Spencer danced away from him, singing a song about pretty girls and the boys who loved them.

"But then you started making these weird sculptures," Mr. Shay said, totally frustrated with the fact that Spencer wasn't listening. "And now you're putting Carly at risk."

Ever since he had seen that hammer fly through the air toward Carly's head, he had been getting angrier and angrier. If Spencer wasn't going to listen to reason, it was time to take drastic measures. He had hoped it wouldn't come to this, but Spencer's behavior convinced him that he had no other choice.

Mr. Shay raised his voice loud enough to be heard over Spencer's music. "So, maybe it's for the best if Carly comes to live with me."

That got Spencer's attention immediately. He stopped singing and pulled the ear buds out of his ears. He was speechless.

"Carly needs a grown-up to keep an eye on her," Mr. Shay said seriously.

"I am a grown-up," Spencer insisted.

Mr. Shay shook his head and snorted.

"And I really don't think she wants to go live with you in Yakima," Spencer said.

"And why's that?" Mr. Shay asked.

"Because she likes to have fun," Spencer told him.

Mr. Shay was insulted. "Oh, you don't think I'm fun, huh?" he asked. He imitated what Spencer had done earlier in their conversation. He pulled up his shirt and rubbed his belly while he made siren noises.

Then he glared at Spencer with an expression that said, "I told you I was fun."

"That was pretty impressive," Spencer said seriously.

"I'll be at the Parker-Nichols hotel, two blocks over," Mr. Shay said. He put his hands on Spencer's shoulders. "I love you, Spencer. But Carly needs a responsible, adult authority figure in her life. I'll see you tomorrow."

Spencer watched him leave. *Could his grandfather really take Carly away from him,* Spencer wondered. A feeling of dread came over him. How would he tell Carly?

He tried to repeat his belly-rubbing comedy bit, but he was too bummed out. Instead of a siren, he sounded like a toy whose batteries were running out of power.

CHAPTER 3

Spencer paced around the loft, waiting for Carly to come home. He thought that if he was more like the responsible adult his grandfather thought Carly needed, Mr. Shay might change his mind. Spencer would try to do whatever it took to keep Carly at home with him. And he planned to start as soon as she got back.

Carly breezed through the door. "Hey, Spence, I'm back with one large Blueberry Banana Blitz," she said.

"Where have you been?" he asked sternly, taking it from her.

"At the Groovy Smoothie," Carly said, taking off her jacket.

"For half an hour?" Spencer demanded.

Carly shot him a confused look. "Smoothies are thick. You can only suck them down so fast."

"No excuses. You're out of control," Spencer told her.

Now Carly was even more confused. "Yeah, clearly I have a problem," she said sarcastically. "I'll check into Smoothies Anonymous tomorrow."

Spencer tried to sound like one of those strict dads some of his friends had had growing up. "When you live under my roof, you live by my rules, so . . ." Spencer wracked his brain for rules. He didn't really have any. Carly was a good kid — she didn't need to be confined by strict rules. "Always try your best. And eat your vegetables!" he said finally.

Carly laughed. Since when did Spencer have to lay down rules? What was up with him? "Okay, are you on some kind of new medication I should know about?" she joked.

Spencer tried to yell at his sister, but then realized he couldn't be that stern, responsible adult. It just wasn't him. "Ahh, I can't do this," he said, dropping onto the couch.

"Do what?" Carly asked, sitting down next to him.

Spencer sighed. "After you left, Granddad told me he doesn't think I'm responsible enough to take care of you."

"That's not true," Carly said. Spencer took great care of her!

"He thinks you'd be better off living with him in Yakima," Spencer explained.

Carly jumped to her feet, panicked. "Yakima?" she yelled. "I am *not* moving to Yakima. He can't do that, can he do that?"

"I don't know," Spencer admitted.

"But you're very responsible," Carly told her brother.

"Our grandfather doesn't think so," Spencer said.

"Well, we're just going to have to change Granddad's mind," Carly announced. "I repeat, I am *not* moving to Yakima."

Spencer could see how upset Carly was. He didn't want her to be concerned. He wanted his sister to be happy. "All right, don't worry too much about this yet," he said, trying to calm her down. "Just go do your homework or something."

"Okay," Carly said. She grabbed her backpack and headed for her room.

Spencer put on his responsible adult voice again, barking like a drill sergeant. "I mean, you go do your homework right now, young lady!" His smile gave him away.

"Yes, sir," Carly said, playing along.

"And just say no!" Spencer added.

"Always!" Carly assured him.

Spencer watched her run up the stairs. "And stay in school!" he added.

Carly grinned at him, then yelled over her shoulder. "Maybe."

Joking with Spencer had made her feel a little better, but by the next night Carly had worked her way up to a panic again. She paced around the *iCarly* studio while Freddie and Sam tried to provide moral support.

"Will you chill?" Sam said. She was hanging out by Freddie's tech equipment, eyeing all the buttons.

Carly had too much nervous energy to stop

pacing. Every time she thought about having to leave Seattle, leave her friends, and leave her brother to live in Yakima, she had to do two more laps around the studio. "I'll chill after my granddad's convinced that Spencer's a responsible adult."

Sam chuckled at the idea of the words responsible and adult being used to describe Spencer. "Yeah, good luck with that." She was upset by the idea of Carly leaving, but she refused to believe that it was actually going to happen.

Freddie was stressed — stressed about Carly possibly leaving and stressed about the fact that Sam was touching his stuff. "Hey, could you keep your hands off my equipment over there?" he yelled.

"I could," Sam offered, "but I don't think I will." She grinned at Freddie and started pressing buttons on his control panel.

Freddie's got to his feet and marched toward her, but his next move was cut off by the *ding* of the elevator. The doors opened to reveal Spencer wearing a very old and very small suit. He looked like a first-grader dressed up for his first piano recital.

"I'm wearing my suit," he said grimly. It was so tight that he walked like Frankenstein's monster.

The *iCarly* team eyed him curiously.

"Nice," Freddie lied, trying to be supportive.

"Isn't it kind of small on you?" Carly asked.

"Yeah," Spencer agreed. "I only wore it once in tenth grade, for a school play."

"What role did you play?" Sam asked.

"Man in Suit," Spencer told her. He tried to stretch his arms out in front of him and couldn't. The suit was too tight and it was cramping his style. "This stinks," he said, totally frustrated.

"You're not supposed to like it," Carly told him. "It's supposed to help Granddad see you as a mature adult."

"Okay," Spencer said, dropping his arms. "But can we have ice cream after he's gone?"

A bell rang downstairs.

"Doorbell," Carly said grimly.

"Smells like your granddad," Sam said. She turned to Freddie. "You smell like garbage."

"Your head's shaped like a ham," Freddie told her.

Carly turned to them. "Hey, no fighting tonight," she ordered. Then she turned to Spencer. There was nothing she could do about the suit now, but that tie looped around his neck needed some help. "You figure out how to tie your tie, I'll go down and stall Granddad."

"Okay," Spencer said.

Carly and her friends headed downstairs to answer the door.

"What do you want us to do?" Freddie asked.

"Get out," Carly said simply. She didn't think her grandfather would appreciate having her friends on hand while they dealt with their family issues.

"Right," Sam agreed.

She and Freddie hurried toward the front door.

"Wait! The back way!" Carly told them. What if her grandfather used the fact that she had friends over all the time as another reason to claim Spencer wasn't a good guardian?

Sam and Freddie turned on their heels and

hurried through the kitchen. Sam grabbed a fruit bowl on her way out. All this stress was making her hungry!

Carly waited for the back door to close. Then she smoothed her clothes and fluffed her hair before opening the front door to Mr. Shay.

"Granddad," Carly said nervously.

Granddad held up a pink T-shirt. "Surprise!" he said.

"Wow. An 'I heart Yakima' T-shirt," Carly said, trying to sound happy.

"For you!" Mr. Shay said.

"Yay," Carly said halfheartedly. She took the shirt from him. "Why did you get me this?"

Mr. Shay closed the door behind him and led Carly to the couch. "Carly, come sit," he said. "I got in touch with your dad last night."

Carly groaned. She had hoped her grandfather wouldn't pull her father into this, but he had. "Aw, man."

"I told him I was worried about you, you know, living here with Spencer," Mr. Shay explained.

"And what did he say?" Carly asked. She was hopeful all of a sudden. After all, her father was the one who agreed that Spencer could be her guardian when he learned he was going to be stationed on the submarine in the first place.

"He thinks Spencer is very responsible," Mr. Shay admitted.

"See!" Carly said happily. "He knows what he's talking about."

"Wait," Mr. Shay said. "Your dad also agreed that since he's not here right now, I can decide what's best for you."

Granddad would decide? Didn't Carly have any say at all? Now she was convinced her father had no idea what he was talking about. "Well, what does he know?" she asked. "He's in the Navy on a submarine three miles under water! He's probably all dizzy!"

"Carly, you're coming to live with me in Yakima," Mr. Shay said firmly.

"No! I want to stay here in Seattle with Spencer!" she pleaded.

Mr. Shay shook his head. "Spencer needs to learn to take care of himself before he can take care of a child."

"I'm not a child! I'm just young and short," Carly said desperately.

Mr. Shay tried to calm her down. "Sweetheart —"

Carly didn't want to hear it. "Spencer's very responsible and very grown-up!" she insisted.

At that moment, Spencer came bounding down the stairs in the suit that made him look ridiculous. "Hey, you guys," he yelled, "I was wondering —"

Whatever he was wondering was lost when he tripped and fell down the stairs like an over-excited little kid.

Carly smiled weakly at her grandfather. This wasn't helping her case at all.

Spencer pulled himself to his feet using the back of the couch. His tie was in a giant knot around his neck. He tried to cover up his tumble by pretending nothing unusual had happened. "Who's ready for dinner?" he asked casually.

Mr. Shay shot Carly a look as if to say, *See, I told you so.*

Okay, so she couldn't prove that Spencer was

responsible and grown-up. Carly still didn't want to leave Seattle.

"Please don't make me move to Yakima," Carly pleaded.

Spencer stood behind her. "Please don't make her move to Yakima," he begged.

Mr. Shay shook his head. "Yakima is a great town," he told them.

"No great town can be named Yakima," Carly said. She didn't even try to keep the disgust out of her voice. "It sounds like someone throwing up," she said.

Spencer thought that was a very intelligent comment. "It does," he agreed. He pretended to throw up while repeating the name. "Yakima. Yakima."

Carly eyed her brother nervously. Once again, he wasn't helping her case.

Mr. Shay crossed his arms over his chest and refused to even consider what they had to say. "I'm sorry, she's coming to live with me," he said firmly.

"Then I wore this monkey suit for nothing!" Spencer yelled, stretching his arms in front of him to show them how uncomfortable it was. His tie was choking him. He tried to rip it off, but he couldn't get the knot loose. "Stupid tie!" he spat.

While Spencer wrestled with his tie, Carly kept trying to convince her grandfather to let her stay in Seattle.

"You're wrong about him," Carly said.

"Look, I love Spencer," Mr. Shay said.

"Then let me keep living here," Carly told him.

"And what if something bad happens?" Mr. Shay asked her.

"Nothing's going to happen," Carly assured him.

Mr. Shay wasn't as convinced as she was. Something bad had almost happened the other night. When Spencer's fan of hammers broke down and that hammer went flying, Carly could have been seriously hurt. "You don't know that," Carly's grandfather told her. "Remember the hammer."

"I ducked!" Carly insisted.

"What if you hadn't?" Mr. Shay asked quietly. He shuddered, picturing that hammer embedded in the wall. What if it had hit Carly in the head?

Carly was near tears. She stamped her foot. "But I did!"

Mr. Shay had made up his mind. There was nothing Carly could say that was going to change it. "Can't you see I'm only thinking of what's best for you?" he asked, heading for the door. He was trying to end the discussion, but Carly wouldn't let him.

She followed him to the door. "No! And what about school?" she asked.

Mr. Shay had already thought about that. "You can transfer to Yakima Junior High."

Carly couldn't think of anything worse than transferring schools. Her friends were in Seattle, not Yakima. "Gross!"

Mr. Shay put his hands on his granddaughter's shoulders and looked into her eyes. "I'm sorry, baby, my mind's made up," he told her gently. "You can have a day to pack up your things and say good-bye to your friends. We leave tomorrow night."

Carly watched her grandfather leave the apartment and turned to Spencer with sad eyes. Spencer had been fighting to get his tie off during

Carly's entire conversation with their granddad. At some point, he had used a wooden spoon to try to get the knot out, and now the spoon was jammed between his face and the tie. He had also managed to get his arm wrapped in the tie and wedged over his head. Spencer was totally stuck.

Carly saw him and sighed.

"Call for help," Spencer said sheepishly.

Carly shut her eyes for a moment, then set about helping her big brother free himself from his tie.

CHAPTER 4

The next day at school, Freddie held a card-board box for Carly while she cleaned out her locker. Sam looked on, still trying to wrap her mind around the fact that tomorrow Carly wouldn't be around — she'd be in Yakima.

"I can't believe you're moving," Sam said, totally bummed.

"Well, believe it, because it's happening," Carly said.

Freddie was mad. He was really upset that Carly's grandfather was making her move away from her friends. "You know, I ought to go tell your grandfather a thing or two," he said.

Even as bummed as she was about Carly's pre-dicament, Sam couldn't pass up an opportunity to insult Freddie. Especially not when he made it so easy. "If only you knew a thing or two," she said dryly.

94

Carly put a few more things in the box Freddie held, then reached for her MP3 player. Sam's eyes lit up when she saw it.

"Oooh, can I have this?" she asked, taking it out of Carly's hand.

"I'm moving, I'm not dying," Carly told her.

"But don't you want me to have something to remember you by?" Sam asked sweetly. "Like nine thousand of your favorite songs?"

Carly rolled her eyes. "Give it," she said, taking the music player back.

"I'm just trying to cheer you up," Sam told her. And it was true. She'd rather have Carly than a music player.

"You can't cheer me up," Carly said. "I'm moving to Yakima. I'm going to be a Yakimite, or a Yakimaneeshin."

"Yakimaniac," Freddie said, proud that he had come up with something.

Once again, Sam saw an opportunity to bug him. "You're Yakimannoying," she said. Then she turned back to Carly. "So, what about our show?"

"I don't see how we're going to do *iCarly* anymore," she said, her voice thick with tears. The

95

three of them had had a blast making *iCarly*. The show got funnier each week, and their audience was growing, too. Carly was totally bummed about the idea of having to leave that behind.

Sam walked a few steps away and faced the wall. The sadness written all over Carly's face was too much for her best friend at that moment.

Carly shook her head and got mad all over again. She had been moving from mad to sad and back again ever since she heard that her grandfather wanted her to move to Yakima. "This whole thing is so lame! So Spencer's a little unusual. Big deal," she said. "It doesn't mean he can't take care of me."

Sam wasn't ready to give up. There had to be a way to change Mr. Shay's mind and stop this disaster. "Hey, what if we think of a way for your granddad to see that Spencer's a good guardian?" she asked.

Carly perked up. "Yeah," she said.

"How?" Freddie asked.

"I could pretend to do something really terrible," Carly said, running with Sam's idea.

"*Riiight*," Freddie said, nodding. "Something that'll get Spencer really upset with you."

"Yeah!" Carly said, her voice rising with excitement. "Then he'll freak out and yell at me right in front of Granddad."

"Which will make him realize Spencer's a responsible authority figure," Sam added.

"I love it!" Carly said. She felt lighter and happier than she had in two days. This would work, she knew it would!

"So what bad thing are you going to do?" Freddie asked.

"I don't know. Let's think of something," Carly told her friends.

Sam grinned. Something really bad was right up her alley. In fact, it was what she did best. "I enjoy this assignment," she admitted.

They all headed for class, deep in thought.

Later that day, Spencer was making Carly's favorite dinner — a Chinese stir-fry with chicken. The doorbell rang.

"It's open," he yelled.

Mr. Shay came in.

Spencer stiffened. He had planned a special dinner for Carly. Just the two of them on their last night together. He didn't exactly want his grand-dad to ruin it for them. "I thought you weren't coming to get Carly until later," he said.

"She called and asked me to come here for dinner," Mr. Shay explained.

"Oh, did she?" Spencer asked. He made no attempt to hide the anger he felt.

"Yes. Maybe she's handling this whole thing more maturely than you are," Mr. Shay told him.

"That's because I'm not mature, isn't that what you said?" Spencer asked.

Mr. Shay looked into the wok to see what Spencer was cooking.

Spencer tried to cover it with his arm. "Must you look in my wok?" he asked.

"I just want to know what you're cooking for dinner," Mr. Shay said defensively.

"Stir-fry chicken. Is that okay?" Spencer asked. He picked up a whole, raw chicken. "Or do you think Mister Chicken should go pack his bags and go live with you in Yakima?" he said sarcastically.

"Will you stop picking fights with me?" Mr. Shay said. "I happen to love you. But I love Carly, too, and as her grandfather it's my responsibility to make sure she grows up with a —"

Spencer cut him off. "You're just mad that I don't want to be a lawyer like you. You're upsetting Carly and me. You peeped in my wok, and you made me touch raw chicken which I don't —"

Spencer's list of complaints came to a complete halt when Carly slammed through the front door. "Hi, guys," she said. She sounded like Carly, but she certainly didn't look anything like the Carly who Spencer and Mr. Shay were expecting for dinner.

Carly was totally punked out. Her hair was dyed three different colors, she wore heavy, black eye makeup, and she had pierced her eyebrow, nose, and lip! She was dressed in black, and wore a black leather choker with metal studs along with black leather boots and black leather wristbands. Instead of a belt, a heavy silver chain was wrapped around her waist.

Carly shocked Spencer and Mr. Shay into agreement on one thing.

"Oh my gosh!" they both said at the same time, rushing over to her.

"Carly! What have you done?" Mr. Shay asked.

Carly was enjoying their reactions. She couldn't wait for Spencer to start yelling. "Well, I figured since I'm going to a new school, it's a perfect time to, you know, reinvent myself." Carly struck a pose. "You like?"

"Like?" Mr. Shay exclaimed. He was totally horrified.

Spencer's reaction was completely different. He didn't freak out. He didn't scream at her like the angry guardian their grandfather wanted him to be. "You look fantastic!" Spencer said.

Now it was Carly's turn to speak in stunned unison with her grandfather. "What?" they both yelled.

Carly realized that her reaction wasn't the right one under the circumstances. "I mean, you really like it?" she asked. She focused her eyes on Spencer and tried to signal him to say no — to agree with their grandfather. Spencer was ruining her plan!

Spencer didn't read her signals. "Yeah, you got the crazy hair and the piercing," Spencer said, looking her over. "It's so in your face. You know, like BOO!"

Mr. Shay thought Spencer's reaction was just one more reason why Carly should live with him in Yakima. "You approve of this?" he asked Spencer, totally outraged. "Have you —"

Spencer shushed his grandfather with a look. "Give us a sec," he said to Carly and then pulled Mr. Shay aside for a private talk.

"How can you think she looks good like that?" Mr. Shay asked.

"I don't," Spencer told him.

Mr. Shay was confused. "Then why'd you tell her —"

"She's a little teenager," Spencer explained, cutting him off.

Mr. Shay still didn't get it. That was all the more reason why Carly shouldn't walk around looking like a nightmare. "But —" he argued.

101

Spencer cut him off again. "You've got to let kids express themselves," he said. If there was one thing Spencer knew more about than other adults, especially more than lawyers, it was about letting people express themselves.

"I always let Carly express herself," Mr. Shay said defensively.

Carly knew they were arguing about her new style. She thought if she let them know it was part of a plan — a failed plan — they would at least stop arguing. "Can I interrupt?" she asked.

"Not now," Spencer told her.

"Quiet, Carly," Mr. Shay said.

Carly went back to the kitchen and slumped on a stool. All her hopes about getting her granddad to see that Spencer was a responsible adult were dashed. She was bummed — big time.

Spencer and Mr. Shay were still arguing.

"Look, this is just a phase," Spencer told him.

Mr. Shay was sure that this new look would lead to even worse things. "And what's her next phase? Stealing cars?"

Stealing cars? Mr. Shay's examples were so

far over the top that Spencer pretended to take them seriously. "I don't think Carly knows how to drive yet."

Mr. Shay shook his head. "This just proves that you are unfit to take care of my granddaughter."

"She's my little sister, and I'm very responsible no matter what you say," Spencer told him. "I know everything that goes on around here."

There was a *whoosh*, and the ingredients in Spencer's wok caught fire. Neither Spencer nor Mr. Shay noticed, but Carly did.

"Uh, guys?" she said.

"What?" they yelled together.

Carly pointed at the wok and the flames that were shooting up into the air. They grew bigger by the second, setting the fire alarm off.

"Fire!" Spencer yelled.

"Don't just yell!" Mr. Shay said, grabbing the phone. "Do something!"

Spencer ran to the fire while Mr. Shay dialed 911. The intense flames spread to the cookbook next to the wok, forcing Spencer to jump away from the flames. He frantically ran around the kitchen looking for something that would douse the fire. In desperation, he finally grabbed a broom and started whacking at the flames.

"Yes, we have a kitchen fire," Mr. Shay said into the phone. "Please send help right away."

Instead of putting out the flames, Spencer's broom caught fire. He waved it over his head, trying to put it out, but that only sent sparks flying around the kitchen. He screamed and threw the broom at the wok before running over to Carly.

Carly was calmer than either her brother or her grandfather. "Don't worry," she said coolly. "We're just going to —"

"Quiet!" Spencer yelled. "I'm saving your life." He threw Carly over his shoulder in a fireman's hold and ran for the front door.

Mr. Shay was still ready to pick a fight. "Careful with her!" he told Spencer.

"Run, old man, run!" Spencer yelled.

CHAPTER 5

An hour later, Carly and her family were in the building's lobby. Freddie and his mother were there, too, along with all of the other people who were forced to leave their apartments until the fire department had made sure the fire was completely out.

Lewbert, the building's doorman, was going crazy. He didn't like people and tonight the lobby was full of them. "Ahhhh!" he screamed, pushing his way through the crowd. "Too many people in the lobby! Ahhhh!"

Two firemen walked through dripping water, dragging their equipment.

"Keep off my floor, I just mopped!" Lewbert yelled. "Ahhhh!"

Sam raced in. Outside a car honked and Sam turned to yell out the door. "Just wait in the car, Mom. Man!"

She walked over to Carly. "Hey, Freddie texted me to say you had a fire," she said. She checked out Carly's punked-out makeup and jewelry. "Nice rods and ring," she said, pointing to the piercings.

"If you like them, take them," Carly said. "I already told my granddad and Spencer they were fake."

Carly took off the fake piercings and handed them to Sam.

Sam didn't get it. The piercings were supposed to help convince Mr. Shay that Spencer was a responsible guardian. Why would Carly confess that they were fake? "Why?" she asked.

"Because Spencer thought I looked good," Carly explained. "Then his chicken burst into flames and now I'm going to Yakima."

Mrs. Benson overheard Carly say that it was Spencer's chicken that started the fire. She stormed over to Spencer. "So this fire is your fault," she said.

Spencer was too sad and defeated to deal with one more person telling him he wasn't a responsible adult. "Mrs. Benson, please —"

"Because of you I had to stop right in the middle of rubbing anti-tick lotion on Freddie."

Freddie cringed. He was totally embarrassed to have his mom talking like that in front of people — especially Sam and Carly. "Mom, I don't have ticks," he said for the thousandth time.

"They hide in your leg hair," Mrs. Benson insisted.

"I don't have leg hair!" Freddie yelled.

"Which really worries me deeply!" Mrs. Benson said, wrapping her arm around her son.

Freddie opened his mouth to respond, but he knew there was no winning this one. It would only lead to a discussion about leg hair — something he definitely did not want to talk about in front of Carly and Sam. He gave up.

"I'm sorry," Spencer told Mrs. Benson. "I was making dinner and it caught on fire."

"Well, you're lucky no one got hurt," Mrs. Benson said.

Spencer shook his head sadly and walked away.

Sam raised an eyebrow and eyed Freddie with an evil grin. "Anti-tick lotion?"

"It's precautionary," Freddie said defensively.

Spencer trudged over to Carly and Mr. Shay. The fire and Mrs. Benson's comments were the last straw. He felt totally defeated. He couldn't take care of Carly. He had almost gotten her killed twice — first with a flying hammer and then with a flaming wok.

"You were right. Okay?" Spencer told his grand-father. "I am irresponsible. Carly should go live with you."

"Spencer," Carly said, trying to stop him. She could see Spencer felt terrible. And it wasn't true. Spencer was eccentric and he could be goofy, but he wasn't irresponsible.

Her grandfather agreed with Spencer however. "Well, I'm glad you see it my way, Spence," he said. "You can come visit any time you like."

Spencer nodded sadly.

A fireman approached them. "All right, the fire's out. It's all clear," he said.

"How's the damage?" Mr. Shay asked.

"Nothing too bad," the fireman told him.

Another fireman walked by with the charred wok. He was eating Spencer's stir-fry with a half melted spoon. "This is some good chicken stir-fry," he said with a smile.

Soon, they were back in their apartment, and Carly was bringing down the last of her things from her room. Mr. Shay waited for her at the bottom of the stairs.

"Okay. This is my last suitcase. I'm ready to ruin my life," Carly said.

"Look, I know you're upset, kiddo, but once you smell that Yakima air, you'll feel better," Mr. Shay told her.

"Yes, the sweet smell of Yakima," Carly said sarcastically. She walked over to her friends.

Spencer came into the room carrying a piece of paper. "Here," he said, giving it to his grandfather.

"What's this?" Mr. Shay asked.

"Everything you need to know about taking care of Carly." Spencer pointed to the paper. "I listed all her allergies, the number for poison control —"

"She has allergies?" Mr. Shay asked, surprised. He didn't know Carly had allergies.

"Yes," Spencer said, pointing to another list

on the paper. "These are Carly's favorite foods, drinks, soups, and chowders."

Mr. Shay wasn't expecting this level of detail. "Aren't soups and chowders the same thing?" he asked.

"No, there's a distinction," Spencer told him. He turned to page two. "This is her homework schedule with the phone number of a good tutor because she's been having some trouble with science."

Mr. Shay looked at Spencer seriously. There was a new respect for Spencer in his eyes, but Spencer didn't see it. He was still focused on the detailed lists and instructions he had put together.

"These are the vitamins she needs to take every day. I only give her the ones shaped like dinosaurs."

"Why?" Mr. Shay asked.

"Dinosaurs are cool," Spencer said simply. "Oh, and she's really into drinking coffee," he lowered his voice so that Carly wouldn't hear him, "but I always give her decaf *but* don't tell her."

Carly was across the room, but she thought she heard something about coffee and decaf. "What?" she asked.

"Nothing," Spencer said nonchalantly. "Keep it," he told Mr. Shay, handing him the papers in his hand.

"Thank you, Spencer," Mr. Shay said, looking over the lists. "This is impressive."

"Wow, thanks," Spencer said sarcastically. Was his grandfather really impressed that he knew these things about his own sister? Of course he knew about Carly's allergies and her favorite foods. Who else would know her homework schedule? Who did Mr. Shay think had been taking care of Carly all this time?

Across the room, Freddie eyed Carly sadly. "So, this is it," he said.

Carly nodded. "This is it." She reached out to give her friend and neighbor a hug.

Freddie tried hard not to cry. "Be strong, Freddie," he said to himself.

Carly pulled away and then turned to Sam — her best friend. She and Sam had done almost everything together for as long as Carly could

III

remember. She couldn't imagine going to school without her. She knew they'd always be friends, but with one of them in Yakima and the other in Seattle, how often would they get to see each other?

Sam tried to joke, but she was just as sad as Freddie was. "So, who's going to take the blame when I put live lobsters in the trunk of Miss Briggs's car?"

Carly chuckled. Sam was always coming up with the craziest stunts. She would miss that. Then she got serious. "Will you at least try to stay out of trouble?" she asked.

Sam shook her head. "Nope," she said sadly.

Carly pulled her friend into a hug.

"Well, we should go," Mr. Shay said, bringing an end to their good-bye. "Long drive, lots of traffic."

"Okay," Carly said reluctantly. "Well I guess I —"

Freddie dropped to his knees and threw his arms around Carly's legs with a tortured scream. "*Noooo!*" he cried.

"Freddie, let go of my legs," Carly said.

"I've got him," Sam told her. She pried Freddie's arms off Carly's legs and helped him to his feet.

"Sorry. Lost my cool for a sec there," Freddie said.

"You can't lose what you never had," Sam joked, but she only half meant it.

Freddie elbowed her in the shoulder.

Carly sighed, wondering who would keep the two of them from driving each other crazy. That had always been her job. But she couldn't do it from Yakima. "Okay, let's go," Carly said, turning to her grandfather.

"Aren't you going to say good-bye to Spencer?" Mr. Shay asked.

Spencer was sitting on the stairs with his face in his hands. Carly and her brother had said their good-byes privately. "We already did before you came up," Spencer told him.

"Okay, then," Mr. Shay said.

Carly turned to her friends. "Will you guys come down to the lobby with me?" she asked. She wanted to be with them for as long as she could.

"Sure," Sam told her.

"Of course," Freddie said.

The elevator doors opened and Carly, her grandfather, and her friends got on with her luggage.

Spencer crossed the room so he could watch her leave. Carly and Spencer shared one last look, then Carly gave her brother a sad smile and a little wave. Spencer waved back. He tried to smile, so she would know he would be all right, but his smile was as sad and lonely as hers was.

Spencer watched the elevator doors close and then dropped to the couch. He listened to the elevator going down, taking Carly away from him, and thought about how quiet the loft would be without her. How quiet his entire life would be without her.

Suddenly he remembered something with a snap of his fingers. "Aw, man!" He jumped to his feet and ran to his room. A second later he sprinted back into the living room carrying an asthma inhaler. "Wait!" he yelled. He had to catch Carly and their grandfather before they left for Yakima!

Spencer hit the elevator button, then realized that would take way too long. He'd have to run down the stairs. He was heading for the front door when the phone rang. Out of habit, he answered it.

"Hello?" he said into the phone.

It seemed that Freddie's mother was still worrying about Freddie's leg hair.

"No, Freddie's not here, Mrs. Benson," Spencer said. "And I don't know when I grew leg hair! I've got to go!"

He hung up on her and ran for the door. "Wait!" he yelled again, taking the stairs three at a time. He had to catch them!

CHAPTER 6

In the lobby, Lewbert was still mopping up the mess the fire department had made on his clean floor. Carly and Mr. Shay got off the elevator, followed by Freddie and Sam.

Lewbert glared at their shoes, convinced they were there to track dirt on his floor. "Ah, more people!" he yelled, totally outraged. He threw down his mop and slumped angrily in the chair behind his desk. He glared at them every now and again so that they wouldn't stay too long.

Mr. Shay ignored him. "Okay, the car's right out front," he said, wheeling Carly's biggest suitcase toward the door. "Oh, young man," he said to Freddie. "Would you mind helping me with —"

"Carly! Wait!" Spencer yelled. He came bounding down the stairs, completely out of breath. "You forgot this!" he said, huffing and puffing. He handed her the asthma inhaler.

"What's that?" Mr. Shay asked.

"My asthma inhaler?" Carly said, taking it from Spencer. Her forehead wrinkled in confusion. "I haven't had an asthma attack since I was seven."

"Well, yeah, but you know, you never know," Spencer said.

Mr. Shay watched the two of them carefully. Spencer's lists and instructions had been very impressive, and now Mr. Shay realized that Spencer knew a lot more about Carly's health than he did.

Mr. Shay eyed the asthma inhaler. "Why did you keep that?" he asked.

"In case she needed it," Spencer answered.

"I'm not going to need it," Carly said, handing it back to Spencer.

Spencer handed it to Mr. Shay. "Take it. Just in case," he said firmly. Then he opened his arms and Carly ran into them for one last hug.

Neither one of them wanted to let go.

Mr. Shay looked at the inhaler, and then at Spencer and Carly. He had been wrong about Spencer. He realized that now. Mr. Shay still thought Spencer should have stayed in law school, and he still thought Spencer's art was weird. But when it came to Carly, he realized that Spencer was definitely adult and *definitely* responsible.

"Nah. I'm not going to need this," Mr. Shay said.

Spencer couldn't believe that. What if Carly had an asthma attack? "Look, asthma's tricky —" Spencer refused to take the inhaler back.

"I'm not going to need this, because I want Carly to stay here with you," Mr. Shay said.

Carly's whole face lit up. "Really?"

"You're serious?" Spencer asked.

Freddie dropped to his knees and threw his arms around Mr. Shay's legs. "Thank you! Thank you so much."

Sam was too happy to speak. Too happy even to insult Freddie at that moment — she'd save her comments for later.

Mr. Shay shook his head with a laugh, pleased that he had been able to make everyone so happy. "Could someone remove this young man from my trousers?" he asked.

Spencer pulled Freddie off Mr. Shay and helped him to his feet.

"Just remember, I'll be dropping in on you guys from time to time," Mr. Shay told his grandchildren.

"Please!" Spencer said.

"Any time!" Carly added. She loved her grandfather. She just didn't want to leave Spencer.

"Because I still think you're a bit of a nut bar," Mr. Shay told Spencer.

"Why?" Spencer asked. "Because I do this?" He lifted his shirt and rubbed his belly, making loud, silly siren noises.

"Don't do that," Mr. Shay said, sounding annoyed. "You do it like this." Mr. Shay raised his shirt and rubbed his belly, howling like a werewolf.

Carly was totally mortified. "You guys are so embarrassing," she said, looking around.

Spencer and Mr. Shay stopped and waited for her to let them have it.

Instead, Carly flashed a grin. "If you're going to do it, do it right!" she joked, jumping in the middle of them. Soon she was rubbing her belly and making bizarre sounds too — a cross between Spencer's sirens and her granddad's howls.

119

Spencer and Mr. Shay added their voices to hers.

Sam and Freddie looked at each other as if to say, *This family is crazy.* Then they shrugged and joined in.

Lewbert slipped down behind his desk, totally horrified.

Carly looked around at all the silliness with a big grin. She had known all along that her grandfather loved her and was doing what he thought was best for her. But she had also known that living with Spencer in Seattle was where she belonged. They needed each other. She was incredibly happy that her grandfather had finally seen that.

Knowing that Granddad planned to visit more often made Carly happy, too.

She was exactly where she wanted to be, surrounded by the people she loved.